*** Predators ***

A six-pack of short fiction

Some predators are animals
Some predators are human
Sometimes it's hard to tell the difference

Cover Design: J Lacy Coughlan
Cover Images: Bill Delorey

Special thanks always to Genie, for her support and encouragement over the years

Thanks
Professor Luke Wallin and Writer Michael Lee
A little piece of each of you resides in everything I write

Thanks to my colleagues
Dr. Fred Bercovitch, Dr. Marc Whaley
Professor Charles Bachman
Their professional contributions in the fields of behavior, biology and psychiatry bring realism to these characters and the biological triggers that rule all life.

Published in United States of America

WordWizard Publications
411 Walnut Street Suite 6317
Green Cove Springs, FL 34748

Additional thriller/suspense novels by this author

*** Shuffle an Impulse ***
by William Delorey
(c) 2015
A psychological thriller and suspense novel

*** Operation Crossbow ***
by William Delorey
(c) 2015)
A military and espionage suspense thriller

<u>Coming in 2016</u>
*** Hobo's Revenge ***
by William Delorey
(c) 2016
A novel of greed and financial manipulation

www.billdelorey.com

This short fiction collection illustrates predatory behavior in animals and humans, and social repercussions when behavior interacts in the wilderness or a tribe or a culture. Language describing scenes in these stories may make it less suitable for younger ages.

*** PREDATORS ***

Lucas Patcher drops another branch on the campfire and sparks fly into the night. Stick figures and shadows dance along the steep canyon walls. Patcher rubs a calloused palm across stubbly cheeks, fingers a bushy mustache, and pours coffee from a blackened tin pot.

Steam rises above his cup, the odor of fresh coffee floods his nostrils. Patcher sips, grunts, pulls his lips away quickly, blows across the hot metal rim and sips again. He settles his back against a rock, pulls a multi-colored woven cape tighter over his shoulders, warding off the desert chill. He pushes an old, beat-up leather hat back on his head.

Barely perceptible in the high desert with no breeze, the arid scent of dry sand and ancient rock hangs in the stillness, mingling with a spicy aroma wafting off sugar pine, junipers, and sage. Within arm's reach, his new rifle leans against a rock.

Hobbled near the spring, a red Morgan gelding stands with his head high, snorting cloudy vapor into the stillness. His muscles quiver when the distant cry of a cougar echoes down the canyon for the second time in the past hour.

Patcher uncoils off his seat and eases alongside the horse, gently patting his rump. "Easy Buster, he's too far away to bother us. But we'll git to him soon enough."

Patcher straightens the blanket over the horse's flanks, rubs his neck and feeds him a carrot. The horse settles down and begins nibbling a few tufts of grass.

The cougar developed an appetite for sheep, raided Patcher's stock about once a week for the last month and last week nearly killed his yearling filly. After four years of drought, the mountain lion methodically slaughters what little profit remains.

Comforting the horse a bit longer, Patcher stares into the darkness and contemplates his ranch, his livestock, and this chore. His wife and children sleep comfortably on a western slope of the Sierras. Steep and majestic, the tree-covered peaks rise between where Patcher now stands and where he lives and works one hundred twenty acres – a small place pushed hard by his family and one hired hand.

Returning to his seat by the fire, Patcher relaxes his back against the rock once more, nodding his head down onto his knees. He needs some sleep, and plans to pack up before daylight for an early start. The fire sinks into coals and Patcher slides beneath his blankets.

*

Six hours later Patcher awakens with a start, snapping his eyes open as a false dawn brightens the horizon. The whistle of birdsong pierces the morning silence and tiny toenails rustle dead leaves beneath the desert brush nearby.

Patcher stands, stretches the kinks out of his lean frame, letting his eyes circle the camp. During the night Buster moved away from the waterhole and rests near a clump of bent willows. Wispy gray smoke spirals upward above the remaining coals.

Tossing in a few twigs, he awakens his fire, picks up the coffee pot and heads toward the spring, pushing his way easily through the thin underbrush. Suddenly, Patcher freezes.

A bloody jack rabbit lies on the sandy bank, quivering and squirming, trying to drag itself away from a female cougar lapping water.

The cat lifts her head, aims her eyes at Patcher and flexes immediately, poised to charge or retreat depending on her whim. Her thick pink tongue hangs above the spring, curled and still. Water drips from her mouth and two amber eyes study Patcher. She elevates her tail, flattens her ears, and digs powerful claws into the sandy soil. The tip of her tail twitches back and forth. Raw strength pulses in a hundred pounds of golden muscle and radiates power into an emerging sunrise.

Breaking daylight barely brightens the terrain. A slight breeze blows between them, carrying Patcher's scent away from the cat and the cat's scent away from the horse. His rifle barrel pokes above the rock, too distant to reach. Almost without movement, his left hand eases over the hilt of his hunting knife, his right still cradles the coffee pot. Patcher holds his breath.

But for her tail twitching, the cougar remains motionless, then a low snarl rumbles in her throat and her lips curl back, exposing deadly yellow fangs. A ridge of hair springs erect between her shoulders. Patcher dares not move a muscle, his left hand hovers above his knife. Sweat trickles along his ribs and his neck itches. One full minute ticks away, and then another.

Patcher needs a bath.

Both predators stare, immobile, eyes locked.

Savage ferocity electrifies the space between them.

Hobbled hooves rattle on the trail behind him and Patcher grunts. The Morgan pushes through the brush and bobs his head beside Patcher. Buster pricks up his ears and blows through his nostrils, jerking his head back when he spies the mountain lion crouching across the spring. Patcher grabs the leather halter and holds the horse still.

The cougar suddenly blinks, snatches the wiggling rabbit in her jaws and leaps backwards, loping down the game trail heading east. The end of her tail bounces above the stunted brush, her head intermittently appearing each time she jumps.

Detouring off the trail where the walls shorten, the cougar bounds into sight and sprints up the steep canyon slope. A darkened silhouette on the rim with the rabbit hanging from her mouth, she glances back at the campsite once then drops down over the ridge.

"Damn," Patcher growls and releases a drawn out breath, "A female, with cubs." His job just became twice as difficult, tracking a mother back to her young. He knows the cat will take live prey only to train her cubs for the hunt, and would eat a kill that small on the trail if she has no offspring. Patcher could have taken her anywhere he found her, now he must find the cubs too.

*

An old and unmaintained forestry road skirts his ranch on its eastern slope then cuts south then east again across the valley floor, circles around the mountains, and rises into the foothills. Patcher had driven the dirt roads across the valley almost a full day to get up into these canyons.

Strong and agile, the cougar climbs straight up and then returns over the ridgeline east of his ranch when she hunts. Much quicker than when Patcher travels the same distance.

He tracked the cougar for three days since. If he fails to locate her lair today, he will waste another day moving his truck and horse trailer farther north.

Patcher continues toward the spring and fills the pot, knowing he now has plenty of time. If he follows the cougar, she will only circle away and protect her kittens. By waiting,

Patcher can track her directly from this canyon back to the den. A few fistfuls of dry brush coax his fire to life, and the smell of bacon frying and coffee perking soon drifts up the canyon.

Perched on a flat chunk of sandstone, Patcher dips a hunk of bread into the plate of beans and bacon on his lap, and stares at the canyon wall where the cat disappeared. He spots movement along the bottom of a low cliff and his eyes focus on a wandering white-tail. The deer takes five or six steps, nibbles, then takes a few more steps, pops her head up looks around then nibbles again. Two fawns drift into sight, followed by another young doe. Between bites, Patcher watches the family idle down to the spring and drink.

"Dinner right here in her own back yard and she still comes after my sheep," Patcher mutters. He sits quietly, reflecting on his family. His wife and twin teenage daughters tend the ranch whenever he's away.

His confidence never flags, but he knows his absence means extra work for everyone. He stuffs the last crust of bread into his mouth, scrapes his plate, scours it with sand, rinses, and packs up. He strips off his shirt and vest, straps on his holster and checks his loads, then carries a bar of soap and a washcloth down toward the spring.

*

Unable to climb the steep canyon wall on horseback, Patcher hikes up to the ridge top, checks the panther's direction of flight and discovers paw prints heading across the gully and higher up the next canyon. He backtracks and saddles his horse. Three hours later Patcher circles out of the canyon and begins trailing back up the next one.

The Morgan moves along at a brisk pace but Patcher slows him when they approach the area where the cat fled earlier. Responding side to side each time the reins touch his neck, Buster tracks back and forth across the canyon floor below the ridge where Patcher last saw the cat, and where he now searches for sign at barely a crawl. He finally spots her prints sporadically disturbing the sand, a flat line appearing between them intermittently where she dragged the rabbit along the ground on several steep sandy inclines.

He tracks the cougar for three hours, losing the trail twice on rocky terrain. She headed east from the spring then turned northwest up into the canyon and Patcher figures it's the nearest water to her den.

Suddenly, a disturbing presence bristles in the dry afternoon air, sending a chill along Patcher's spine. His hunter instinct and experience picks up an indefinable sense of life hovering in the wilderness. Hobbling the Morgan near a patch of grass, Patcher grabs his binoculars, rifle, and a light backpack, hooks a canteen on his belt then sets out on foot.

Two extremely careful hours later Patcher eyes a steep, angling draw with a shallow cave dug under a scrub bush growing on the hillside above it. He adjusts his binoculars and the scene settles into focus.

Packed dirt flattens the trail where it enters the den and decaying bits of animal remains dot the hillside. One cougar kitten lies dozing, its head resting on a dirt mound at the mouth of its den. Another cub sprawls beside it, gnawing a chunk of bone.

Patcher lets out a breath and settles in to wait. A hundred and fifty yards he estimates, too far for a shot, and if he moves closer in daylight, he'll expose himself. He decides to watch until the cougar ranges out for her nightly hunt, and position himself for her return. The half-moon will provide enough light. Patcher pulls a ration bar out of his shirt pocket and takes a bite, leans back against a tree stump. Content, he doses in the late afternoon sun.

Two mottled cubs scuffle and spar for about an hour. The mother cat finally climbs out of the den and stretches. She lifts her nose into the breeze, testing, bright yellow eyes survey her domain and a wide yawn exposes four deadly canines. Both cubs attack her. She cuffs them playfully, gently wrestling, her coarse tongue licking each in its turn.

Patcher watches through the glasses until dusk. Jagged shadows crawl across the canyon floor and the sun drops behind the rocks. The cougar chases her cubs back into the cave, bats each one back inside as one or the other attempts an exit. A half hour later, she emerges alone and trots down the draw.

Three hours after sundown the moon sheds dim light on Patcher while he works his way above the cave and in line with her trail out. Sheltered by a scruffy tree, he huddles between two boulders fifty feet below the mouth of her lair. The rifle aims back along the trail, its barrel resting across a low bush. His handgun lies beside him on a flat rock supported by gnarly tree roots protruding from the sand. Patcher waits.

*

Three hours pass. Buster whinnies into the breeze several miles down the canyon and jolts Patcher alert. "Come on kitty, come to poppa," Patcher whispers. He removes his hat, placing it on the ground beside him.

Rotating his head slightly, he stares over his shoulder along the rugged, meandering trail. A crisp dawn backlights the canyon rim. He sees nothing but darkness. He hears nothing but silence. Twenty minutes pass. A soft bleat sounds behind him and a little to his right.

He eases his head and shoulders around and spots the cougar sixty feet away. Patcher squats between two boulders beside and above the trail but directly in line with her approach to the cave. The cat returned along an unexpected route over the ridge behind Patcher instead of coming up the trail where she departed earlier.

The cougar stands on a rock ledge above Patcher and carries a fall lamb. The lamb squeaks a tired, frightened bleat and weakly kicks its feet. The cat studies the terrain surrounding her lair, but has not seen Patcher.

Anger pulses through the rancher when he spots his lamb, and mingles with a fear the cat might see him and charge before he can react. He remains still as a stone but grips the gunstock. Hefting its weight with one hand, he slowly rotates the rifle and aims it toward the cat.

The cougar balances on a large jut of rock then crouches briefly, preparing to leap onto the trail directly above where Patcher waits. Suddenly, her eyes blaze in recognition and she releases the lamb.

Another pain-filled bleat disappears into the diminishing darkness as the lamb tumbles down the hillside. The mountain lion curls back her lips exposing sharp yellow fangs and a terrifying scream erupts from her throat.

Leaning off balance, Patcher quickly swings his rifle the few remaining inches, squeezing the trigger when the barrel lines up with her chest.

The cat launches herself off the rock ledge, every muscle stretched for the kill. The gas cartridge hisses and white smoke escapes when the hammer strikes the firing pin. Embedded deep into the cougar's throat, the shot leaks blood and stains her chest but she hits the trail running directly at Patcher.

He jerks sideways, the sand gives way and he drops his rifle, rolls between two boulders and over a low bush. His fingers clutch at the pistol, knocking it away as he slides past the flat rock it lies upon and tumbles fifteen feet down the rocky hillside, landing on the canyon floor below.

A sharp pop splits the air as the knuckle above his wedding ring snaps, and his left ankle twists beneath him. Scrambling erect, he balances on his right leg and awkwardly spins around, seeking the mountain lion and his weapons.

The wrenched ankle supports his weight but begins swelling almost immediately. Splinters of pain shoot across his wrist and up his arm. A deep cut on his cheek leaks blood into his week-old whiskers and another abrasion stings his right ear.

The cougar caroms off a tree stump and, weakening, swipes at her throat. She swings her head side to side and tries to focus on Patcher. She growls when she sees him, but then her eyes glaze over. She swats at her chest again, staggering.

Her final attempt to lunge buckles her knees, and the cat sags and lies down on the trail above Patcher, breathing heavily. Eyes vacant, she stares down at him, her tongue lolls sideways, flicking dirt.

When the cat finally slumps, a grim smile of relief crosses his face. Patcher slouches against the bent tree trunk, panting, his body shakes with fear and excitement, adrenaline pumping strong into his bloodstream. Sixteen times over the past twenty years he hunted the cats, protecting his stock, his neighbors' stock, or under contract with the rangers. It's never easy, and tonight is the closest he ever came to losing.

Patcher pushes himself upright, limps over and attends the lamb. She struggles and climbs to her feet on the canyon floor, scratched, cut, and shivering. Her eyes focus on Patcher while he examines her injuries. "Damn laws are gonna git me kilt."

He cradles the lamb in his arms and struggles up the

hill, sets her down and grabs his pack. He splints his broken finger, nearly passing out when he jerks the bone straight. He cleans and disinfects the cuts, draws his knife, hacks off his boot and wraps his ankle, then pulls three wool socks over the swelling. He leans back and rests a minute breathing heavily, intense pain sapping his strength. Finally, Patcher gathers his nylon ties, strings the cougar's paws together and bags them, then muzzles her head.

Morning sun peeks above the ridge top, splashing golden rays across her tawny fur. Shallow breathing swells her chest and a strong heartbeat punches evenly against her ribs.

The cougar broke the feathered head off the dart, but its plunger emptied the barrel into her bloodstream. The quick-acting narcotic rendered her unconscious. Patcher peels back her eyelids, checks her pupils then examines her entire body. He injects a longer acting drug into her rump.

"Take all damn day to git 'em back to the ranger station, too," he grumbles. "Cain't even shoot 'em no more."

He locates his pistol in the underbrush, retrieves his rifle and reloads, then hobbles up the draw to collect the young cougars. Patcher grabs a tree branch and hauls himself up the embankment. Both kittens hiss and spit at his approach then slip backwards into the cave.

*** Poker Face ***

One by one the cards hit and slide across a felt cover. The dealer builds a neat pile before each player. Everyone gets five. "Seat three leads," she holds the deck low, hiding the bottom card each time she shuffles. The game is five-card draw, and no one looks at seat three.

Seat three is a shill, a house-man, I think. He changes tables often, keeps the action moving when it slows, and appears whenever a table holds less than four. Not something you'd notice unless you come here often, as I do, and he never seems to win much, or lose, just keeps playing. If I'm right, the house backs his losses, up to a limit, and he keeps half his winnings.

Shill peeks at his cards.

We begin the ritual, delaying the inevitable as long as we can. The hand plays good or bad, and nothing will change it until we draw. I steal a glance at seat five, fingering my cards into a tight stack.

Seat five waits, bowing her head as if prayer will guide her and she must be last to know. She peeks over bifocals at each of us, cards untouched, hands busy with matches. She exhales and smoke hovers above the ante, then drifts away. Wattles of flesh dangle beneath her chin and a road-map of years etches time on her face, leaving dents and channels where streets would be.

She looks a hundred, but smiles as if she enjoys it, and the cards, especially the cards.

Grandma holds up a glass, rattles the ice and grins at the hostess. "Scotch, rocks. Please." She beat me on a couple of tough hands earlier, two of the largest pots, and some of the chips now in her pile arrived in my pocket earlier. She smirked at me both times, and I hope I smirk back at least once tonight.

Impatient to begin, my hands rest over my cards, fingertips tingling, tapping a rhythm on slick plastic. My thumbnail slides under one card and lifts its corner. A one-eyed jack stares back. Hidden behind tinted glasses and shaded from overhead lights by the brim of a straw hat aimed at the ante, only my eyes rotate toward seat four.

Seat four looks like a student, or a jock, a lifeguard maybe. Sunburn radiates above his collar and along thick arms protruding from the sleeves of a tee shirt stretched tight by his frame. He sits quietly, never wastes a move, picks up his cards all at once and fans them behind his palms. His mouth remains a thin line below a thick mustache, but his eyes dart about trying to catch others looking, always pausing when they hit mine, as if trying to figure me out.

Lifeguard flirted a few times when he sat down, but gave up when I ignored him. He drops his cards, memorized, and sips tea he brought in a sack. The club supplies hot water, and the hostess offers to freshen it. He nods yes, but never says a word except when he bets or calls for cards.

Five cards hit the stack of chips, face down. "I'm done," says the man filling seat six, his shortest sentence all evening. He leans on the table, and I wonder if it might tip. He pushes to his feet. Sweat trickles along his jowls and his shirt sticks to him. He's been losing most of the evening, removed his coat and tie earlier, and tried to sell insurance between deals.

No luck there either. Might have done better if he'd kept his mind on the game, but he'd combined poor selling attempts with bad cards and even concentration won't help if you don't get a draw. Tried to sell me some until I told him I had a law degree, married a doctor, and don't need any because we give at the office. The lies shut him up.

A seven hides beneath the corner of my second card, a heart, same as the jack. Another peek, another heart, a king this time. The tingling slides along my arms, a battalion of hair snaps to attention, three hearts to a flush and I struggle not to. I'd beaten a guy all night once because the hair on his arms stood up and his eyes dilated every time he held a good hand. Since then, I've always worn sleeves draped to my wrists, tinted lenses I don't need, and comb my bangs long above my eyes whenever I play.

Blood sings in my veins, a tiny chorus of yes, yes, two more hearts please. Seat one is empty, and now seat six. Four players, it's late. "Seat three, your lead," the dealer demands, "open or pass."

"Open." Shill drops his cards then rubs his palms over faded tattoos stenciled on pencil-thin arms that look like they've never seen sunlight. His five-dollar chip circles into the pot, and he sips coffee at least an hour old. He doesn't worry me much, the house takes two percent of each pot, rounded up to the dollar, and his job keeps the pots open and active. He plays okay, but never a threat. Just not good enough or he'd never shill, he'd play instead.

Wordless, Lifeguard blinks, sighs, and tosses a green chip on the pile.

Grandma finally looks at her hand, studies her cards, and hides behind her fingers. She peers through the tops of her bifocals, then the bottoms, as if it might change the patterns. Her face remains unreadable, she's done this before.

We all know it, doesn't change anything though.   "Raise."
She tosses a red chip on the pile and retrieves two green.

The insurance salesman departs. I quickly check my
last two cards. My possible heart flush disappears with
another king and jack. Two pair, I fight a grin. "Call."

The tingling pumps up to a steady pulse now, as this is
a fine hand to draw. Thirty dollars left, table stakes, I never
bring more than a hundred and always leave my credit cards
home.

It's a twenty-five mile drive each way and I usually
won't if I need more cash. A bad night doesn't get better if you
throw money at it. There are times I've won over a thousand
in a single night, but I've never lost more than a hundred
except once, two years ago as a rookie.

Made a mistake. Brought a checkbook and credit cards,
lost twenty-five hundred and got home just in time to shower
and leave for work. And piss off my husband. He made me
pay it too, course I wrote the check out of our account – big
deal.

Shill calls, tosses a chip and a card on the table. "One."
His new card floats to the felt.   Must be drawing two pair,
or three with a kicker, but didn't raise - three would raise. Or
could be an ace with a joker to the flush or straight. He opened
though, needs a pair at least.

Lifeguard drops another chip and holds up three
fingers. Must have a high pair. Barely moving her hands, the
dealer stacks three neatly in front of him.

Grandma sucks on her cigarette, tosses her discard, and
a cloud of smoke shapes a ring and surrounds the word,
"One."

Half the tables sit empty, and the twenty-odd in use are
not crowded. Slow for a mid-summer Thursday in Reno.

"Well," I say, "three ones, and a three," and smile, hoping I can again when the hand flips over. No one responds.

Shill looks at his draw. "Check."

Scotch slides down her throat like water, ice tinkles against the glass and her teeth. Grandma bets, two green chips hit the pot. "Ten." she says.

Squeezing cards won't change the spots, but Lifeguard tries just that and stares, then frowns. He slaps the cards down, stands, grabs his tea sack and chips, glares at me up and down once then struts away without a sound. Still wishing.

I slide my new card under then pick up my stack. Another king. My heart thumps and I hope no one hears it. Sounds like cannon fire to me. Tiny hairs stand up beneath my collar, but a bandanna wrapped around my throat hides the hint. My fingers spread the cards, just to be sure. I peek. Full-house. Kings and jacks. 'Yes!' echoes in my head. I want to smile at Grandma but don't, and work hard keeping it calm. A good hand, a great hand, and the last for me tonight. Might break me even, down seventy bucks.

Of course, it's never the money. It's always the contest, the rush, the strategy, the thrill of competition. It's never the money. "Raise," and kick two black chips into the pot.

Intoxication, addiction, the high almost orgasmic, love of the game sends my blood racing. I hide it. Ten dollars left and wish I had more, maybe. I'll know in a minute. Grandma drew one, to a straight or a flush? Unlikely, not with a raise before the draw. Even three with a kicker is okay. Only one full house in the deck can beat kings. Lifeguard stayed with a high pair, so could've had aces. Then her best full house'd be smaller than mine.

Shill tosses his cards. "Fold." He rests his forehead on his palms, as if lost and whipped. Probably is, house rules suck the life out of shills. No future.

I glance at my wrist. Ten to midnight, I'll be late. Grandma signals the hostess, lifts her glass and nods, returns her attention to the game. "Table stakes," she says, "raise your last ten." Her eyes twinkle behind thick lenses as if she's teaching me a lesson. And knows it.

For one fleeting second, I wish I'd broken my rule and brought more money, just to see if her look changes with another raise. Motionless, but vibrating on my chair, I flick my last black chip into the pot, grinning. Her eyes don't blink, but a smile quivers at the edge of her lips then spreads across her face. Again. She turns up four threes, but I knew I'd lost as soon as she smiled.

The hand is set before it begins and we all just go through the motions, but I always wonder if anything I do gives me away. Just as well I'd brought no more money. It's twenty-five miles, and my husband likes me there to greet him after work. The hand broke me. Grandma rises with me, nods at the dealer, and leans on her cane toward the ladies room.

I drive around and brake in front of the building, idling a moment. Grandma pushes through the glass entrance. I kick the car door open and help her sit. She pulls out a pile of money, and hands me a stack of bills, half my losses.

"Drop me at your mother's," she says, "I'll stay the night, what's left of it anyway," then turns toward me. "Your eye twitched when you caught that last king."

She laughs, then I laugh, and the tires chirp, spinning away from the curb. "Don't tell mom I was out with you again, okay Gram?" I plead.

*** COUNTRY JUSTICE ***

Rejecting big city life and all its back-stabbing struggles, Mikki Toner drives two days nearly non-stop, napping in the blacktop pullouts whenever he feels his eyes droop. He finally angles in off the highway, bumps across the tracks, bounces in a few potholes, rambles down a dirt road, and lights up his brakes. The old green pickup squeaks on its springs and settles in beside the oak hitching post some townsfolk still use for its original purpose. Horse tying.

Mikki rolls his wrist and rotates a crank. The glass disappears inside its panel. No fancy electronics in this old classic. He sticks a paw outside, pushes the lever down, kicks the door open. "Gotta git that fixed," reminding himself for the hundredth time. Ain't lazy, just can't find parts.

Stretching out a few road kinks, Mikki inspects the view down Main Street, only road through town. "Ain't much different." Same old dirt road, same old potholes, same old hitching post, same old Meeting House Bar.

Little park at the south end pops a couple oak trees and patches of grass outta dry red dirt and faces the eastern slopes. A few Ford pickups sit on a small lot beside it, for sale signs stuck in each window. A new business.

A cool breeze blows in off the lake, pushing out the heat and scattering crisp brown leaves across the fields. Couple dust devils dance in the dirt. Mikki climbs up one step and strolls along the boardwalk, convinced he'd gather all the history he missed in a single day of chatting. Come home a couple times these past few years too though, so ain't much he missed. Not a lively town here, that's for sure.

Unraveling his memory a bit, Mikki recalls that final good bye right before he hit the road, aiming himself at a life beyond what eighteen years and his future here conceded. A mental video lights up his brain, his own personal matinee replaying those final moments.

*

Dottie Toner and Billy Savage stood in the road waving good luck at his rear view mirror, watching that green Chevy tailgate disappear in a cloud a dust. Dottie tucked her curly red hair right in under his chin, spilling a few tears onto his shirt, and Billy Savage fulfilled his last six birthday wishes all at once, hugging Dottie Toner. Put a smile on his face and a lump in his jeans doing it too.

*

Not such a great trip though as it turned out, not like Mikki expected anyway. Six years gone sour, but now he's back. Good old country boy for sure, coming home.

Mikki catches the door swinging shut and steps inside behind an older male wearing a slouched hat and a nasty scowl. Old man drops four dollars and grunts beneath a bushy upper lip peppered with a few gray strands, "Gimme one, Joey," staggering a bit for so early in the day, like it ain't his first trip here. Or his second.

Stout, white-haired guy behind the bar pours a double jigger full. Old man swallows it off and points at it again. Bartender shakes him off, drags the bottle back, sticks it on a shelf.

"Enough for today."

Mikki points a grin and a finger at Joey, tips his fist and sips like he's hiding an invisible draft beer in his palm.
Bartender nods his chin up and down, smiling, grabs a mug and pulls the tap, reading Mikki's signal.

Joey hollers over Patsy Cline fallin' to pieces on an old jukebox. "When'd you git back?"

"Just now. Two minutes."

Kid sitting at the counter stares straight across at a mirror glued to the wall behind the servers bar, watching its reflections. Recognizing the mean old face coming right at him, the kid twists a frown onto his lips and wishes that image belonged to someone else. Those nasty old eyes'd burn a hole right through a chunk a coal without needing a match. Wrangler jeans and pointy-toed boots caked with slick red mud slip up behind him.

Ice cream dribbles down his chin, drips onto his new t-shirt. Kid sucks at it, tries to wipe it off quick, hide it from the angry gleam aiming itself at him. Too late.

Old man slaps the kid sideways off his stool. "What you lettin' that drip for? Clean shirt don't need no ice cream drippin' on it," the old man barks. "Where'd you git that dollar? Steal it outta my jar?"

Kid looks up at what he knows coming next. Fright sparks his tears quick as a blink. The old man hovers above the young boy, unbuckles his belt, slips it out and raises it behind his shoulder, begins a downward whack.

The belt wobbles, stuck like a fish hook caught in a tree. Mikki holds the buckle in his left hand, wraps the leather once around his wrist, braces his right hand against the bar, and growls, "You ain't big enough to whip a youngster without this here strap, then you outta be ashamed a your weak-ass self."

Old man snarls over his shoulder, "Ain't none a your business."

Mikki sets his feet, tugs on the belt a bit, keeps the old man off balance. A weak and spineless man without it, whiskey turns the old man aggressive and meaner. A ten dollar bill and change buys him a bit of liquid courage as long as it lasts. A few hours usually, then peace in the house for that hour or two a pass-out keeps him on the couch. Some folks claim, 'it's in the water', a taste of false big-shot and a kid-beater gene, though not everyone gets it.

Pretty tough in his day, but most of that wore off over the years. Still got some fight in him despite the gray streaking his hair, but mostly bluff and bluster, same as early in his life. Intimidating when he gits away with it, easing off quickly when he don't. Hiding himself from the hurt often comes his way when alcohol replaces a better idea and he mistakenly picks on someone his own size.

Old man shifts his weight, gets himself ready. Mikki senses the movement, anchors his body and leans a knee into the thin old thigh. "Don't push it, Alvin. I ain't a youngster no more. Y'all start it, y'all wish you didn't."

Cowardice sits in his brain, a normal occurrence all his life. Alvin relaxes his grip then releases the belt and steps one pace away, installs his everyday malicious and nasty face. "Why'd you care anyways? Ain't your brat."

"Uncle's close enough, Alvin. Still family. Touch leather to my nephew again and y'all answer to me directly. Don't give a damn you live with his gram, don't make you his kin. Git on home and sleep it off. Take it out on Maggie or my sister again I'll be comin' for you later. Believe it."

Mikki glances down at the boy. "Git up Pickles, he ain't hittin' nobody today, not for an ice cream drip he ain't."

Alvin takes a long hard look at Mikki, runs his eyes up and down, evaluates the new muscle and the old confidence he remembers too well. Figures he'd lose this one, maybe all from here on if he ain't careful. And he ain't never careful, just a bully whenever he gets away with it. The old man turns on his heel and stomps out the door, stumbles as he hits the boardwalk, bounces down a step and lands face-first in the dirt. Gets up cussing, slams his hat back on his head and rambles down the road, dusting off his pants.

Mikki watches Alvin wobble away then leans down, grabs a hand, pulls his nephew upright. "Come on Pickles, git up here and eat your ice cream 'fore it melts."

"So, where'd you git that dollar anyways? Don't abide stealin' no more'n I do beltin' a kid."

"Didn't steal it, earned it." Pickles points big brown eyes at Mikki, fortifying his truth. "Drug and stacked six bales into Mrs. Friar's barn. She bent a leg, limpin' some, needin' her horse feed put under cover. Got no husband now."

Pickles pulls up his shirt-tail, sniffles and wipes his cheeks. "Fuck it, Mikki, got tears on it now, snot too. Might as well throw it away as keep it." Pickles grins up at his uncle, giggles.

"Ha! Mom'll wash it out tomorrow, be good as new. Alvin'll never know it."

Mikki laughs out loud and ruffles the dark red curls on the twelve-year-old boy that resembles himself and his sister, but thinner. "And watch that word around Dottie too, she won't be washin' out nothin' but that mouth."

"Huh?" Mikki says. "Perry Friar gone? Didn't hear that yet. Pretty young dude."

"Yup. Two months ago. Died milking that big old Holstein, one with the white face and fat black shoulder stripe. Forgot how mean she was? Don't like cold metal on warm tits in a warm barn. Some kick, some don't. She kicks, hard and every time. Gotta hobble her, we all know it, Perry too."

"Didn't hobble her, not that Sunday. Leaned in grabbed a tit, stuck her in that milker tube, cold steel hit that udder and the hoof kicked like a cannon ball shot off a boat. Lifted Perry right over the curb, landed crooked on the water trough. His back tweaked, bad tweak, couldn't move hardly."

"Got no ambulance here, Grip McCarthy took him. Terry loaned him a new Ford, full a gas too. Grip's truck too old for seventy-eight miles runnin' that fast on mostly dirt and gravel. Then somethin' got Perry in that county hospital ... split vein bleedin' into his brain."

"Doc missed it and the surgeon too. Lookin' at his back instead of his head. Busy clinic. Too many people takin' names, not enough docs fixin' folks."

Mikki nods his agreement. Accidents happen, no one at fault. Busy ER, doing jobs fast, even good doctors miss stuff. No reason to hang 'em for it. Doctors human, like other folks, just read more, know more things about bodies and germs.

"Saw it myself, Mikki. My new job whenever Perry milked, sweepin' up, and took cows back. Hosed 'em off, locked 'em up in the outdoor corrals."

Pride puffs up his chest, Pickles first real job after delivering papers before school three days a week. Papers don't count, just collect quarters, wasn't a real job, least not like the Perry Friar cow job. Actual paychecks come with it. No insurance. No retirement.

The boy and the man step outside together, heading on over to see Dottie and Maggie, then on to Granny's General Store, buy Pickles an extra shirt, then come back for a drink and maybe another sundae. Find friends and gather up family for dinner. Meeting House the only eating place in town.

Pickles smiles at that thought. More ice cream.

"Lost my job though. Mrs. Friar shot that cow, butchered it up and stuck it in her freezer. Sold the other nine to Jake Jenson. Gives her free milk when she needs it, put it in the deal. Kids all growed and gone anyways."

Mikki tosses the fancy buckle and tooled leather belt into a wood barrel showed up one morning years ago at the edge of an alley runs between the bar and the sheriff's office.

Looks like an old oak wine cask, two rusty metal bands wrapped around it, but no top. Even got a cork hole, no cork. Folks mostly put trash in it instead a littering. Once started, got to be a town habit and never stopped. A good thing. No one remembers when, it just appeared. Became the main greeting at Meeting House, and still is occasionally. Seems every conversation began, 'Ever find out who brung that wood barrel here?' ... and ended, 'Nope.'

A thing to ask when you ain't got nothing to say but want to contribute. Friendly enough question while Joey Holmes lets white fizz settle atop your draft. Right before that god-almighty first long thirst-quenching sip you earned squatting and walking and riding in the dust all day at the farm or the ranch. No other jobs around. That's exactly when you need it most, and exactly when Joey Holmes sets it right there on the bar with the froth still bubbling, like it's been hiding inside that cold keg all day just for a guy to git here. Mighty tasty suds.

Grip McCarthy started hauling that barrel off to the dump and bringing it back empty whenever he headed that way for his own business. Been hauling it ever since it appeared. Must've been part of his mayor campaign 'cause as long as people remember folks been calling him Mayor Grip too, and laugh, even though no one recalls any election to go along with his title. Somehow he gets a small paycheck off the town taxes too. Must know somebody.

Keeps this town clean, exactly the way he wants it despite the dirt roads. Grip started cleaning up when he lost his job at the Kipper Ranch. Grip started liking Tom Kipper's daughter.   Might have been all right just by itself, but trouble was she started liking him back - been liking him back longer than Tom knew it. Been liking Grip longer than Grip knew it too.

Ellie Mae Kipper carried a crush on Grip McCarthy home every day since she was in grade nine and just began blooming. Long about her hitting her senior year Grip noticed that flower opening up just about right and a sweet young scent following her around as well. A scent that tickled his nostrils exactly how nature designed it.

By that time Ellie Mae already been hooked on Grip McCarthy in secret for a whole three years, and some. Waiting. Watching. Hid behind a tree one day back then, typical young gal of fourteen admiring older boys. She knew he was hers when she saw that bright red cowboy shirt. First time she laid eyes on it was brand new, and he took it off so it'd stay dry along with his old blue jeans.

Story goes, Jimmy King was hanging out with a hook and a worm stuck in the water down Pencil Creek. No luck. He was hungry and pissed he caught no fish that morning. Kicked a bullfrog off its stump and into the water. No good reason.

Grip McCarthy slid on over behind Jimmy King and shoved him off the foot bridge and into the creek, joined him up with that frog he kicked. Then stripped off his clothes, folded 'em into a nice neat pile, jumped in himself. Jimmy King and Grip giggling and wrassling in the water, having a buncha fun after that first push.

Frog got hung up in an old wire fence all crinkled and crooked along the banks. Grip untangled the frog and set it right back on that old stump. Ellie Mae behind a bush, staring between her fingers, embarrassed grin on her face looking at boys with no shirts or pants.

Grip put his new red shirt and old pants back on. Bullfrog sat there a minute, croaked twice and hopped off into the creek nice as you please, and without no thanks unless that croak counts. Crawled back inside the wire mesh puzzle where it felt safe. Saving a frog ain't worth nothing, seemed at the time. Grip just laughed. Wrong thinking as it turned out.

Sure worth something though, for sure. Ellie Mae fell in love. Grip didn't even know she was alive.

Patient gal, not many of them around nowadays, not farm living gals anyway. Watching boars, bulls, roosters in the barnyard, and ole Skitters chasing all the bitches every spring, soon as season hits and heat swells 'em up. Skitters runs all over town, nose in the air, his dick following right along. Got a mind of its own.

Predictable as the sunshine arrives after a cold, sleety winter, Mrs. Elliott taking a box of mutt puppies exactly sixty-six miles down the highway into Wal-Mart parking lot. Convincing some kids they need one before the moms come out the store and catch her angling that new puppy smell and her personal sales pitch. Got it down pat.

She'll chop the head off a chicken and de-feather it in a hot minute, toss it in a crock pot even after her kids name it. But, she can't abide drowning the puppies, gets all hung up in that new puppy smell herself. Always got good luck finding homes though. She don't give up.

Early education about life and ranching, and young gals best learn it right now or y'all be pushing out the baby bump sooner than y'all planned it. Not such a great idea.

*

Old Alvin pushes up off a wood bench in that small town park where he's been sleeping a drink off, catches his balance, staggers into the General Store. Granny and her daughter sitting, chatting, drinking lemonade. Old man picks up a bottle, pulls out a twenty, sets both on the counter. Granny punches the register. "Joey cut you off again, Alvin?"

No answer. He picks up his change, stuffs it in a pocket, bumps against the door jamb on the way out, both sides. Twists the cap off and takes a long swig, turns down the pathway running toward the south edge a town past the Ford lot. Stops and tips the bottle up every three or four wobbles.

Sally sips her lemonade. "There's goes a man this town don't need. Should've let me send him away last time. Dumb move, Leon giving him rehab. Three times. Useless waste a services and county money."

Granny grabs up a shotgun, points an eye along its barrels, aims it at Alvin stumbling down the road. "Be better somebody shot a hole in him. Scoop out all that misery and mean. Pitch what's left of him atop that fresh fertilizer pile out back. He'll fit right in." That gets a pair a giggles. "Sucker needs a bath too." Granny flicks on the overhead fan.

*

Tom Kipper wants no truck with a regular work-hard dude for his only girl child. Not an uneducated ranch hand anyway that only knows how to feed hogs and rake manure, unless he owns the place. Grip owns nothing. So Tom ran Grip off. More'n once before it stuck right on him.

Didn't stop Grip though, didn't stop Ellie Mae neither. Just made 'em sneak around 'til she got older, got a job at the General Store and began bossing herself instead a letting dad do it. Money talks.

Then, course the town grew bigger. Even got a paved road coming part way out when the State and Feds dammed up the north fork near Oak Creek to get more water and power for the government center a hundred and some odd miles west. Got a business no one expects in a town this small. Truck sales.

Terry Madison comes over the Meeting House from Oak Creek most weekends, tips a few cocktails and feels important. Rich guy. Drinks here 'cause no one can stand him at Oak Creek where he lives. Bought the old Patterson parcel in town a while back after Gimpy Patterson died. Knocked the cabin down, left the barn standing, stuck a few Fords trucks on the lot. Gave a piece a land to the town and built that little park. Got a tax break for it, and got warping the business license a little to fit. Started selling pickups. Nothing else sells local. Needing a helper to wash 'em and keep the lot spiffy, Terry hired Nicky Wells.

Nicky Wells. 'Never quite right in the head', folks said, 'Always tinkering with stuff.' Dropped out a school few years ago after tenth grade because he can't learn right from books. So his paw gave him the old mower. Told Nicky, 'Prove your worth son. Fix it and you got the lawn and garden job at the Feed Barn in town.

Wells family owned the Feed Barn ever since Peggy Sherman first set a vegetable stand beside the road. Eleven years old then, now she's Peggy Wells and grandma to Nicky and his two sisters. Still runs the Feed Barn most days, daughter Emily helps her, like a manager.

Nicky took the mower apart, put it back together same afternoon, ran like new. Fifteen years on earth and this kid just got that knack with machinery. Nicky kept that Feed Barn lawn and garden job three years. Mowers, whackers, mulchers, all them power tools ran perfect.

Then Terry paid Grip to remodel the old Patterson barn a little, put in new the windows and doors, build a couple parts shelves and a counter. That's when Terry hired Nicky, couple months later. Sent him to the Ford dealership and trained him some.

Mechanic over Oak Creek said, "Never seen nothing like it. Kid took to fixing a truck like he designed it himself." Magic Touch. Took over all the little repairs back here in town, oil change, tires, like that. Nothing electronic, any big tricky repair or warranty gets sent to Oak Creek Ford.

Terry Madison. Born right near here at the Crooked Fork family ranch, but his two brothers run it now after Terry took off and made a bunch of money in the city. Hated getting manure on his boots.

Nobody saw Terry for years. Came back driving a new Ford pickup, fancy leather package on it, satellite radio and all, still wearing a suit, a tailored one. Terry gave himself a new Ford truck every year. The window rolls itself down, showed everybody his teeth as he paraded it around town, six whole blocks plus the park. Then hit the Meeting House, tossed drinks around like he'd fired up that old whisky still all by himself.

Only did it because he wanted folks to like him and let him stick around. Folks didn't like Terry much, too obnoxious and full of himself but he bought drinks, made up for it. Put that over-wide car salesman smile on his face everyone knew wasn't real. Even Terry. Otherwise all the farmers and ranchers had to drive all the way to Dover for truck service. Ford shop's closer.

Seventy-eight miles one way or forty some odd to Oak Creek Ford, and that's Terry too. So folks put up with Terry and used his tire and oil shop. Plus, Nicky's a nice kid and deserved work.

Friendly kid too, ain't got a mean bone in him, just slow at books and reading. Doc Potter says his eyes might see letters backwards. Can read numbers fine though. Counted his cash out every week and never let Terry short him. Terry didn't dare try it. Paw Wells'd kicked Terry's ass clean off the planet if he'd paid Nicky short. And machinery? Show Nicky once and he got it, every time. Weird.

Dottie Toner's been target shooting, deer and game bird hunting with her real dad all her life, well first twenty-four years anyway, 'til the last six with no dad after Jake Toner got throwed off his horse and broke his neck chasing stock that run off when a freak thunderstorm blew the barn open.

Lightning spooked 'em good and the stock trotted off down Mineral Canyon. Nasty place to catch 'em, steep and rocky, slick in that muddy wash-out. Big mistake riding that stud horse only green-broke, but both geldings and three mares run off with the cattle. No choice.

Surprised everyone though, him a champion rider and all, a likeable guy, husband to Maggie twenty-four years. Dottie popped out five months into the marriage. No shotgun though, they'd been planning a wedding already a year. Mikki showed up six years later. Good father, Jake was. Solid provider, two nice kids, won medals and prize money at the state rodeo every year. Broke neck finished him off though. Only forty-five years a life. Go figure.

Few years later, getting lonely and aging a bit, Maggie Toner took up with Alvin Hardy. Big mistake, but he fooled her. Talked nice, big smiles, held her hand, took her to the Meeting House for dinner every Friday. Danced with her whenever Jimmy King picked his guitar and Boot Higgins fired up his fiddle. Then Alvin twisted back into his real self, like faking it first to get a reward he don't deserve. Maggie.

*

Dottie slams the door, stomps across the porch, and bumps up against the railing. Pissed off don't even come close.

Need madder words, angry ain't good enough. Burr stuck under her saddle blanket ain't good enough neither. Wisp a light brown hair blows across a dark red bruise above her right eye she knows'll turn purple later. Don't need no mirror, been here before. Mad as hell, blood dripping off her chin, tears leaking down a cheek. Left eye swelling shut. No tears on that side. Last time for it.

*

Waiting for his family, Mikki just finished pointing out the window at his old pickup and telling Terry if he'd buy a Chevy instead of a Ford, he'd only have to buy one truck instead of a new Ford every year. Paw Wells, Tom Kipper, Grip and folks sitting at the Meeting House Bar all laugh at that one, including Terry. No one mentions guys living over Oak Creek push his Ford into the Snake River once in a while, just to piss Terry off. Then laugh about it behind his back. Terry just buys himself a new truck after.

*

"No more chances, Alvin." Dottie's voice got a mountain's worth of anger and grit in it.

Alvin turns half around to glare back at Dottie, waves her off like she ain't nothing, then turns back front ways just as she pulls the trigger.

Forty-four forty caliber hand-loaded kicks like a mule. Even her two-fisted grip blows that barrel near straight up in the air. Bullet tears a hole clean through his shoulder blade, misses all the ribs and pops out his chest two inches below his left nipple. Spins off into the dirt somewhere.

Surprises the hell right outta Alvin. Wide-eyed, he rotates real slow, like a smoked hog on a vertical spit tipped sideways, but sure fighting his end. Alvin aims his eyes at a bloodstain spreading across his brand new shirt-front and then at the pistol Dottie Toner drops in the dirt.

*

Everybody at the bar hears the shot. "Nicky probably popped another tire," Grip says, and everyone laughs again, ignoring it.

All eyes turn back to the mirror, watching themselves drink. Terry buys a round. Ellie Mae McCarthy takes hold a Grip's arm and smiles a reflection back at him, happy as a kitten in a lap. Her belly-bump pushing out about half-way now, a little Grip coming. Pickles sticks a spoon in his second ice cream sundae, grins at himself licking it.

Alvin ain't smiling, just laying face up in the dirt.

Not believing it's over yet, his miserable life and him mad most of it, he blames everyone but himself for his failures. His final alive action watches Dottie turn her back on him and walk slowly toward the house, bare feet kicking up dust behind her.

His eyes slide shut. Never will believe it now, Alvin won't. Too late, he's toast.

Be lucky if townsfolk don't just toss his ass off a cliff and let the coyotes have at him. Keep 'em away from the stock one night at least. If he don't make 'em sick first. Got brothers somewhere, maybe they'll take him, save him from the dogs and coons. No one likes Alvin Hardy much, and Maggie Toner just forgives him without thinking the wrong of it. He lies and she believes it. Hopes for a new truth each time when it ain't there. All over now.

Dottie opens the door and walks inside nice as you please. Leaves the gun laying in the dirt right where it fell. Done its job, no more use for it today. Ain't her gun anyway, belongs to her brother. Grandpa Toner gave it to Mikki years ago, an old Colt from Charlie Toner's marshal days before this town was even a town.

Takes her sweet time and all, shuts the door but don't lock it. No need now. She pops open the fridge, wraps ice cubes in a towel, holds it up against her eye, tending the bruise. Important things first. Slips two small chunks in her mouth and groans but ice helps numb the pain and slows bleeding.

She gazes out the over-sized front window Grip McCarthy sold her and her mom couple years ago, and then installed on a handy-man day when he skipped the mayor job like he always done when he gets a labor job from a town resident or merchant.

A big window, solid and clear, no frames except around the edges. Can see pretty near the whole main street if you look an angle at it and push your nose up against the glass just right. Meeting House sits up near the north end.

So Dottie rubs ice, dries tears, wipes blood off her chin, and looks out that big old window. No more kid beating. No more Dottie beating neither. A good work day today, bleeding out an asshole that deserved it every day since he learned how to walk. No more Alvin.

She smiles, a big one, using fat, puffy lips she got from a punch she should've ducked but never saw coming. First one today. Second punch broke same two front teeth as last time, expensive caps this time. Third punch she went and got the gun. Sweet smile anyway, little crooked but she earned it.

Dottie tells the window, "Fuck you, Alvin."

Finally pokes number one on her speed dial, no hurry though, not any more. Perfect shot. "Call me. Important. Don't wait a week neither."

She sets the phone on the counter, wraps her fingers around a cold beer can and rolls it on her spit-lip, pulls it back quick. "Damn that stings." She slides over and stands in front of the big front window. Alvin still lying out there, motionless.

"Is he dead?" She asks the window. "If still he got life in him, lemme shoot that sucker in the nuts if he gits up off the mud 'n dirt 'n blood. Like him to know he'll be arriving in hell without 'em. See if that nasty son-of-a-bitch gits a chuckle out a that one for his mean-ass funny lookin' self."

Nice thought, get another turn at him ... but she'd never miss a cowboy that nasty. Bullet hit that pervert like a magnet sucking lead. Dead-eye Dottie folks'd call her, or Magnet-Momma. Name like that now, how can she lose? Get famous. Open a shooting gallery like Buffalo Bill Cody or Wild Bill Hickok, one of them pioneer shows years ago in the history books now. Annie Oakley too. Ought to get a reward for cleaning that rat off the streets. Maybe Deputy Dottie instead. She grins. A drop of blood hits the floor.

Phone grabs her attention. She pops the tab on the Miller Light, takes a sip, sticks the phone on her ear. "Bout time, Billy Savage. Nappin' instead a workin', as usual. Better git your butt on over here." She plops herself in a chair, leaks out a couple more tears. "Nope, not your pajamas, it's only four o'clock. That all you ever think about? Git dressed and bring your badge too. Just shot Alvin and he ain't gittin' up ... Nope, never."

Gold shield hangs off his deputy sheriff shirt, un-tucked, its tails droop down over his regular blue jeans. Feet bare, Billy Savage stands in the dirt looking down at Alvin, a few stress lines on his face. Worried.

Dottie bounces between sobbing and laughing, and smiling, and bleeding, and tears. A real mess. Mad wins it though.

Dottie Toner hops down off the porch, opens her fist. "Think these two teeth be enough evidence Billy? Want me to knock out another one myself, so y'all can match it, and be sure that's my blood on his knuckles."

She tosses a stack of papers at his feet. "Damn court order keepin' him from hittin' folks don't mean nothin' if it don't come with a deputy attached and followin' us around all day. PAPER! What good is it 'til AFTER he done it again. Mom too. First. Blacked her eye again."

"Jeeeez, Dottie, y'all shot him in the back. How's that gonna look?" Savage wraps his hands behind his neck, pulls a bit, like wrasslimg with a bad idea. Always rubs it when he hits up on a piece of bad luck. And this one's definitely a piece of bad luck. Stamps his feet in a circle, confused as hell. "Damn, Dottie!"

"Hollered at him Billy. Chased him out the door. Just kept walkin', wouldn't turn round and face it. Waved a finger at me instead. What else was I gonna do? He was gittin' away." Dottie climbs up on the porch, kicks at a chair like it sassed her or something. "Alvin earned that bullet Billy, clear as day got sun. Got no grief in my heart for it, for him neither."

"Jeeeez, Dottie, if y'all just shot him in the front, I maybe could do somethin'."

"Well, talk to Sally Parker, she wrote that worthless paper. Sure kept him away, didn't it? Like she and Leon did those other times and left his sorry ass out the jail. Tell Leon we just gave him some extra rehab, a little hot lead toppin' it off."

"Right. Hey, Judge Parker, y'all gotta let Dottie go. She just gave old Alvin a little rehab. Permanent rehab, which he sorely needed." Savage laughs despite the body lying in the street. His feet keep circling the drain, kicking up dust, wrapping his arms round his head like he always done when he stressed up. "She'd laugh us right out the court, even if she is a cousin on my mom's sister's married side ... Somewhere."

*

Judge Sally Parker. First child a Granny Parker who owns the General Store. Single mom once, Granny was. A teenager in trouble. Granny never told Grady 'til years later. Young, on his way to college then, full scholarship and all. No sense telling, forcing him.

Granny just left town, hid out with family, birthed Sally at age seventeen, came back and kept her secret. Whole town pried at it for awhile but she never told. Married Eli Parker a year later. Opened the store together and Eli took Sally like his own, adopted and legal.

Then Granny gave Eli three sons, and now seven grandchildren. Got the name Granny early since the third generation arrived so early in her life. No one calls her anything else, even Eli warmed to it after awhile.

A smart farm gal, Sally grew up local but then snuck away. Years later Grady paid for her college once Granny told him. Another secret.

Sally came back after a few long years in the city as assistant D.A. Old country blood lodged too deep in her veins. Came back to stick all those country boys in jail for at least a weekend. Get a little revenge for 'em picking on her growing up. Kids 'em all about it though, and tells 'em, "No fine for speedin' Jimmy. Two days and fifty bucks for pullin' my hair in fourth grade." Then flashes her shiny white teeth at 'em.

Sally came back a real beauty too. A few big city dollars and a country heart'll do wonders for crooked teeth and weak eyes. Citified gym time didn't hurt her neither. Shook that stocky butt right off her. Too bad she don't like men. Nothing wrong with that idea in itself, 'cept a few cowboys hanging around asking her to party down on a Friday evening at the Meeting House, and after it too, maybe.

Nice guys too, hard working, wondering why she keeps telling 'em no. Fat chance. All got the wrong plumbing.

*

Billy Savage installs a serious look on his face, points it at Dottie. "Even if Leon bought it, which he won't, and even if he was your old high school spark, but even if he did, and he won't, and Porky too. Y'all still got to shoot him in the front Dottie."

"Could do it now, won't bother me none. Be easy enough, got three more bullets. Gun still layin' in the dirt." Dottie hops off the porch, kicks a boot. Alvin don't even twitch. "Won't bleed no more though. Could squeeze him maybe."

Doc Potter finally rolls up and slides out the old Dodge station wagon townsfolk bought at auction, converted to a body wagon. County Coroner written on the side. Gets minimal use. Town keeps it at the volunteer fire station, right beside Porky's sheriff car. "Called Porky. Ain't comin'. He's over Oak Creek arrestin' Karl Crawford for growin' pot between his corn rows again. Man don't never learn."

Doc been around long as anyone, except his college time. Works at the county hospital, and makes house calls. Not many like that left. Earned a basketball scholarship at state when TV made colleges rich instead of the players. Oddest thing, only five-eleven and skinny as a stick. But that kid could swish a hoop from anywhere half-court and in. Just natural born talent worth a degree at any college.

TV revenue paid winners, not losers. Grady Potter won, that's all it took. Difference was, Grady Potter has a brain too, smart like no one expects a farm boy. Learned to be a good doctor, then came back home. Die-hard country boy, for sure.

Grady breaks out his little black doctor kit. "Let me look at you first, Dottie. Alvin ain't goin' nowhere." Doc spends a few minutes with the eye and her cut lip, packs the jaw. Two teeth gone.

"Think y'all can tell folks he got shot in the front, Grady? Shore help Dottie out. And me," Savage says, his voice squeaking a bit.

"Dunno. Let's take a peek. Alvin's a worthless fuck anyway. I'd shoot him myself if I could figure a good reason to tell Porky and Leon. No sense in Dottie's life gittin' hurt too. She just brought a little country justice to it. Deserved it anyways, surprises me Maggie ain't shot him herself months ago."

"Come on. Let's sit him up before he gits stiff. Dottie can just shoot him in the front, same place. Then I won't be lying, can say he got shot in the front. Ain't no one else ever gonna see Alvin dead but me anyways. Aim it a little down Dottie, like the first one aimed a little down off the porch. Stand back a bit, don't git powder on his shirt." Pretty smart doctor, Grady Potter. "Don't worry about Judge Parker. I'll be talkin' to her myself."

And that's how Dottie Toner kilt Alvin Hardy and never got arrested.

*** LITTLE BEAR ***

We remember an odd journey in the days before white settlers arrived and the warlike bluecoat army had not yet poisoned our land. A young Cheyenne spirit boy lived in a village edging the Great Plains and rising upslope beyond a forest stream that drains snowmelt off the Black Hills.

Fifteen annuals beyond his birth and much stranger than a twin brother and sister his birth mother bore two harvests before him, the spirit boy shared a family lodge in his village lands.

Screaming and slapping at spooks and demons in his lodge each night, the spirit boy drove out evil devils that haunted his soul, protecting his village while his tribesmen slept in safety, all knowing the spirit boy carried his courage and spirit strength into the forest each morning and traveled the Pointing Pathway east into the sunrise once darkness departed and his lodge brightened. Well after defeating the demons that lived in his head each night.

The boy entered his sixteenth turn at four seasons passing on the night a bright sky lit the tribal plantings. Spring blossoms finally chased away the chill and on the first full moon of a new growing season, the young boy prepared for a journey he will embark upon alone and seek his warrior name.

The youth must win his totem spirit before the colored leaves next gather beneath the maples and birch that decorate the Black Hills above his homeland. He showed his tribe a face much braver than he felt, but chose the killing game despite his fears.

Carry home a vicious carnivore, feed and clothe his people, and earn that totem as his own - the toughest choice of all tribal rituals. The boy gathered courage and filled his breast, defeating the fright that at first infused worry in his heart.

The young boy packed his roaming pouch, collecting luck tokens and health omens his tribesman offered, and a spear, bow and arrows, and his favorite stone knife. The boy departed north before the great orange disk climbed above the hills that first spring day of the new annual in the Red Horse period.

The sun rose and set twenty-six times before the spirit boy hauled a young male bear across the stream bed and into the village center. Thin grasses twisted into thick strands held the bear tight on twin birch saplings bound together with matching grass bands. The tribe welcomed the returning hunter, dancing and chanting, cheering for the meat and its heavy winter cloak.

But a strong heart beat rhythmically in the small brown bear lashed upon the litter, and the young native hunter denied his tribe a feast.

The spirit boy pushed away his kin and stood beside his trophy, protecting this grizzly cub he rescued off its hiding tree near a mother bear the gray wolves killed and ate. A deep red slash lay across its nose, and swollen rips in its belly leaked ugly poisons that slowly drained its life.

He entered a lodge at the village center, trading the medicine woman three eagle feathers, two pure white stones, and six black walnuts for a poultice that drained the killing juice. The boy cut away matted fur, dead and dying skin, disinfecting the rotting flesh with black tea and spruce pitch and special potions the witch woman mixed. He hummed the spells she taught. The spirit boy saved the young grizzly instead of eating it and wearing its coat or sleeping beneath it.

He nursed the cub back to health, feeding it thick broth he cooked down from venison hearts, vegetable roots and wild fruit, adding powders and chants the eldest witch woman provided. As if it adopted the spirit boy as its father, the injured cub followed him everywhere the boy journeyed until the moon rose full again and the bear cub healed completely.

The small brown bear immediately earned the name Scarface. The youngest children christened it quickly and raced behind it, slapping its powerful haunches with thin switches in passing, and tagging its stump tail.

Giggles and squeals filled the fields when it rolled its head and growled back at them. But its lips remained soft and playful – sharing its bear smile. In its great heart, the grizzly knew these children only gamed with it, accepting the bear cub as a blood brother with the spirit boy and claiming its strengths for the clan.

The boy and the bear cured the infections and Scarface gained weight quickly, gorging itself in the lush valley filled with berries and fish. At the village center, spirit boy huddled with the tribal chief. The boy explained his wishes then crept unseen into the forest.

The village chief admired the spirit boy and accepted his odd ideas. The chief shut his eyes and asked advice from his own wolf spirit briefly, then ordered a bear dance after the meal chant that same evening such as the spirit boy requested. But the tribal chief added a naming ceremony so the boy may know his name and claim his totem.

Climbing the rocky bluff behind the village, the spirit boy sat and watched his plan unfold. The tribesmen tied the bewildered bear to a stake, danced around it, yelling at it, slapping it, poking it with blunt sticks and firebrands, scaring it so the grizzly will never again come near, making Scarface fear humans again.

The spirit boy and the elders wanted it gone, back into the wilderness where it belonged. Scarface must learn to hate and fear men again or another clan might take advantage of its ignorance and kill it then steal its soul and use it against the Cheyenne. The young boy squatted on a large rock atop a nearby hillside a distance from the bear dance lesson and grinned at the abuse. Even his youthful wisdom told him it will save the bear not harm it.

At the peak of the bear dance a naming ceremony occurred, and forever after all native villagers called the spirit boy Little Bear. Tribesmen released the knots and quickly drove the young grizzly across the stream and out into the Black Hills.

Confused by such hostile behavior the bear retreated into his birth land, hurt and sore from the poking sticks, and frightened by the screaming and beating. Although the savage people it played with as family chased it out, Scarface returned that night after the large orange disk crawled behind its mountain peak. The young grizzly slept in a hollow it found beside a large stone that lay beneath the spreading pines.

Later in the darkness, Scarface hunkered down on a rocky outcropping behind the oaks and watched the village sleep. Its ears twitched each time Little Bear screamed his rage into the dark night. Scarface snuffled quietly and licked its body where the blunt sticks bruised its hide, serenely exhibiting its stoic patience.

When the sun rose again, Little Bear strode past the camp corrals and hopped over the stream bed, departing on another hunt. The grizzly cub slid down the rock onto a path behind it and lumbered along beside Little Bear, as if guarding or guiding or both.

Months passed and winter approached. Demon visions materialized in his mind day and night now, and spook voices barked in his brain while Little Bear and Scarface consumed the hunting seasons. Little Bear ran trails, jumped streambeds, and climbed trees and rocks, killing the echoes and erasing the visions that tortured his mind and ravaged his spirit space.

Little Bear chased Scarface up and down the valleys and over hills and peaks, a fierce game of tag they played between them, the boy wrestling the huge bear in the sweet green basin, gaining strength while copious sweat-water leaked from his body and pushed the demons out.

True hunting brothers, the pair shared berries, roots and fruit, and Little Bear often tracked and killed raccoon, rabbit, elk and moose with his bare hands, a bow and a knife, or a stone-head spear.

The great brown bear tracked beside his soul-mate. Six inch daggers adorned his huge paws and muscles much stronger than its prey bulged beneath the thick brown fur.

Little Bear carried madness and power into his hunts and on the warpath, and a rage into battle and into his village that none had seen before.

Daring expeditions into the hills and forests alone without fear earned Little Bear a status above his kin. The tribesmen celebrated his adventures and elevated him to an honor held by a single tribesman in the clan until death released that title and a new warrior claimed it. Little Bear earned the title Warrior Chief, and led the tribal war dance and all its excursions into battle.

Campfire stories filtered new tales of bravery into folklore and spoke his daring deeds across the flames, offering praise and glory for his fearless exploits into the wilderness.

Little Bear claimed that Warrior Chief status with superior hunting and savage combat. Single-handed and alone without Scarface, Little Bear tracked one warrior each in three enemy tribes, defeating a Sioux, a Comanche, and a Kiowa, counting coup and stealing one fine young horse and all their weapons in the time the moon god traveled one full cycle through the heavens.

But still the evil demons ate his brain bit by bit, reducing strength and battle memories he called upon to assist him when confronting the tribal enemies and testing his powerful spirit and the totem he claimed as one with Scarface.

Scarface never entered the village again, but the great grizzly wandered near whenever Little Bear slept in his lodge. The large brown bear accepted the long sleep each time the forest began its freeze but emerged with spring rains, hunting beside Little Bear for three seasons in each annual passing, aging together as one.

Squatting on a rock knob overlooking the village camps, its large pink tongue flapping in the breeze, its nose uplifted, Scarface tasted the fresh spring air continuously in search of the single scent that emanates only from its brave spirit brother and truest hunting companion.

A slight thinness in his flanks and gauntness beneath his chin evidenced his winter hibernations. Patient as a stone, Scarface sat on his paws awaiting Little Bear on the first sunrise of the new growing each of the seven annuals that Little Bear survived beyond the season he earned his name and embraced his spirit totem.

Frequently, Little Bear foreswore the safety of his hut and spent much of his life roaming the forests, hills, and valleys, his spirit totem by his side. Many fathers offered, and the Warrior Chief finally took a wife. The beautiful the young maiden called Running Deer frequently shared his bed despite the demons, but never bore his child.

Inside the sleeping village on the darkest moonless night of all the harvest weeks, we once again heard screams and raging in his lodge while Little Bear fought the demons then departed before the sun rose, taking those evil spooks with him so his village remained safe.

Rain and lightning filled the skies, and one dark and cloudy day during the eighth annual beyond the bear dance and his naming ceremony, Little Bear passed quietly into the spiritual kingdom of forever departed warriors.

No one saw Scarface again at the Cheyenne village and all believe it chose the departure of its bear spirit that same night and joined Little Bear in his great blue sky cave.

The small brown bear cub grew into a huge and powerful grizzly but remained Little Bear's companion for all his earth life, and both still hunt side by side in the hereafter, protecting his tribal families from harm. Two spirit shadows forever wander the clouds, watching over and protecting his few remaining villagers - the Cheyenne tribesmen - who now hunt and farm a modest reservation at the northwest edge of the Great Plains that lies below the Black Hills.

Occasionally, the sky darkens, a flint sparks, and the great grizzly growls. Little Bear and his furry brown totem still battle evil hauntings in the heavens, protecting the tribesmen from devils that live beyond the storm clouds.

Today and forever after, Little Bear and Scarface share a hearth inside the bright blue sky cave nearly two centuries past the night both shed the Cheyenne lifestyle and entered the world of spiritual essence.

Little Bear and Scarface still fight the phantoms that attempt to conquer his people. Cheyenne folklore claim that if a warrior stands tall in the valley below the Black Hills on a clear night with no wind and listens carefully with two ears, he hears Little Bear scream and Scarface roar while the haunting spooks fill with fright then turn tail and flee south toward the driest deserts, escaping the fury of Little Bear and Scarface.

*** FAMILY VALUES ***

Thomas twists the ornate glass knob and pushes gently then puts a shoulder to it. The door creaks open on old rusty hinges, an agonizing squeal fills the landing. Bright mid-day sun penetrates a gritty film on three dormer windows and lights the scuffed hardwood floor, warming the dust. An elderly, well-dressed couple stands in the doorway examining the oddly dimensioned attic where they often played together as children.

"Well, it looks the same except for the dust. Nobody's been up here in years. We better hire Alfie Jorgenson to clean up and catalog when we take title. Looks like someone put everything up here for storage. Rest of the house is empty," Thomas says.

"Do you think we can save it?" Her tone expresses happiness and hope, her bearing and presence hint at aged beauty cloaked in a stream of years, and bleeds elegance on everything she touches. Abigail peeks into the room, smiling at her childhood memories.

"Yes, I think so. The Historical Committee offered a nice pledge for restoration costs if we buy it, but nothing toward the purchase. Grandpa's estate covers nearly half our offer and we'll pay the rest," Thomas replies.

"But do we have enough? Jonathan's illness took nearly all we'd saved, and developers always spend a fortune to buy whatever they want. Can we buy it back, I hope?"

"We'll bid higher than Cromwell can and still remain commercially viable. Profit's his only motive, and you know how Everett is."

She nods, "Yes, I certainly do," remembering the skinny, Cromwell boy who had lived across the creek and aggravated everyone as a teen, and hasn't outgrown it even at his age today.

"We, Abigail, are driven by sentiment and therefore allowed to become financially frivolous. Emotion always clouds capital judgment, my dear." Thomas mimics the stuffiness of a distant uncle that always triggers laughter in his sister.

She obliges. Amusement lights her face and her eyes crinkle deeper at the corners, her giggle dancing on the musty air. "I'm so glad you could come. I really need your help."

The couple enters the attic, picking a path around antique pieces and family clutter. Thomas pushes an old spinning wheel and it wobbles crookedly on its hub.

Abigail gathers her skirt lifting it above the mess. A thin ankle peeks from beneath her bunched dress and would embarrass her in the presence of any other man. Thomas flips out his handkerchief, dusts a spot for each, and sits, palms resting on his brass-knobbed walking stick. She eases down beside him on an old toy box their father built from the packing crate of a cast-iron tub. She had written Thomas of her idea and of the land auction this afternoon.

"Imagine Thomas, a museum dedicated to your music.'

"No, no Abby, something much grander. We'll dedicate it to teaching children the history of music and to our great-great grandfather in the house he built."

"Accordion was the only music he ever played. At least that's what grandma's stories told us."

"Yes. And I still have it," Thomas reflects. "Grandma always said her great-grandfather enjoyed life most when he played and the whole family danced."

"It must have been wonderful. I wish we could have heard him play. Your musical talents must have come from him. We'll display her diary as part of the exhibit too. She claimed he was the only one in our family that played anything, until you and your piano came along."

"Purely by accident, my dear, we happened to grow up next door to a piano teacher, a mere coincidence of lodgings."

His mimic renews her tinkling laughter. "Well then, I'm glad we didn't live next door to an outlaw."

Her gaiety echoes in the room, coaxing a smile to her younger brother's face. Thomas stretches his arm around her shoulders, hugs her frail body, and kisses her cheek. He stands, glances once more around the attic, and moves toward the door. "Come on Abby, it's nearly auction time."

He offers a hand and helps her rise, and they walk arm-in-arm down the grand stairway. Descending onto a landing, admiring the superb craftsmanship of balusters, railing, and the parquet flooring worn thin in places by years of footsteps. Square-head nails fasten tiny oak tiles to a solid sub-floor throughout the house.

The couple ambles along the hall, glancing once more into each of six large bedrooms. Torn and faded wallpaper, cracked panels, broken hinges and an empty double doorjamb give stark clues to neglect over the years. Oak wainscot decorates one wall, open on the opposite side to the stairwell with its carved protective railings, and leads them to a turn atop another stairway, this one wide and curving as well and again fashioned of oak.

A stained-glass window at the stairwell landing draws dim rainbows across the peeling paint. Two broken panes stand watch over weed-choked fields where gardens once grew. The tired old barn sags near a cluster of gnarled apple trees, bent with age and barren from lack of care.

Abigail pauses a moment and gazes at the barn, lost in memories of stolen moments in the hayloft denying amorous boyfriends the fruits of her passion. Her reminiscent smile waltzes across decades. No one has lived in the house for twenty-six years. Uncle Jack inherited then deserted it in 1893 to chase his fortune in the West. The town took possession for overdue taxes. No one rented it and the house fell into decay, but maintains a magnificent undercoat beneath the ruin.

"Only three acres left, the rest was sold off by the town, and built upon. This is the last open space inside the town boundaries," Thomas says.

"Hope we have enough money." Abby looks briefly to the heavens for help.

"The bank appraisal tops at sixty-five hundred. We have eighty-five hundred available, including Grandpa's trust. Even if Cromwell bids it all, we can top him. Hard to believe he'd pay more than its value, even if he does want to build a general store here. And imagine Abby, he actually plans to sell automobiles on the back portion. He must be getting senile. Automobiles, of all things, why not horses? At least horses don't stink."

"I've always thought he was senile, even as a child. He had such odd behavior, cramming his head into books all the time and playing such horrible tricks on all of us," Abigail reflects.

"Until Starkey thrashed him so soundly that time for lighting his sister's hair on fire. Everett hardly spoke to any of us after that."

"You shouldn't have laughed so hard, Abby." Thomas grins and Abigail envisions Everett Cromwell with his face in the mud crying after Starky finally beat him for his pranks.

The steps wind down the stairway, ending on a landing. A set of carved oak doors open off the entry hall and allow access to a huge formal living room. The sliders hang half-open and one dangles crookedly on its track. A wide fieldstone fireplace stretches floor to ceiling along the opposite wall.

Thomas and Abigail wander into shadows beneath the stairway and pass through a wide arch into the kitchen, pausing on its flat, slate floor. Two brick ovens huddle in one corner. The rest of the room lies bare. Both step outside and follow the rambling porch around front, noting several broken windows and split pine railings deteriorating in the weather.

"Well, looks like we'll be alone. You haven't heard from the others?" Thomas asks.

"No, nothing at all, except a note from Justin's chippie saying he's off in Colorado somewhere 'investing' and she'd forward our letter. Kate and Benny don't have much anyway. No wonder, living in Missouri of all places, and with all those children. No telling if Justin even knows."

"Yes ... Justin." Thomas strokes his mustache. "Nothing from him personally?"

"A short letter, about eight months ago, but no response to this idea. The incorrigible rascal cavorts all over the country, carousing and gambling instead of settling down with a nice wife and giving me more grandchildren. Claims he's an investment banker now. I wish he'd act more like his father, rest his soul."

"My God! What's this country coming to? A dandified gambler claiming to be an investment banker of all things. Might find it difficult to love him so much if he wasn't my son." Nostalgia tickles the corners of her mouth, turning the ends up in contradiction. They stand shaded by the front porch, and Thomas glances down the road.

"Well, here comes the town clerk, right on time, must be the auctioneer with him. Wonder where Cromwell is?"

"Mark my words, Thomas. He'll likely not miss it."

As if to punctuate her statement, a tall, thin man steps from the post office doorway. Steel-rimmed spectacles perch on his nose and a tailored suit hangs on his body. Random wisps of gray hair straddle the top of his head. He walks stiffly with his chin in the air and peers beneath his glasses at the world. Puffs of red dust rise in the street behind each gangling stride.

The group gathers in the yard and stiffly exchange greetings. The auctioneer climbs the steps and reads aloud his rules and the auction laws applying to this sale. A crowd clusters behind the fence, a small grouping of townsfolk. The auctioneer raps his gavel and rattles his spiel. No one understands a word until he says until, "Bid opens at thirty-five hundred. Anyone?"

Cromwell jumps on it as if stuck with a needle. "Yes!" He hollers and looks around, hoping he's the only bidder.

"Do I hear four thousand?"

"Thomas raises his walking stick, hot sunshine glinting off its polished silver head.

"Five thousand." Cromwell does not wait for the auctioneer.

"Five," the agent acknowledges, peering at Thomas. "Do I have six?"

"Six thousand, five."

"Seventy-five hundred," Cromwell bids well above the appraisal and a smug look scurries across his face.

Thomas turns and lifts an eyebrow toward Abigail. "Didn't think he'd go above the value," he whispers and raises his voice again. "Eighty-five hundred."

The auctioneer opens his mouth, but Cromwell interrupts. "Ninety-five hundred," Cromwell almost screams, his voice cracks and he aims a glare at Thomas.

Thomas glances at Abigail, at the ground, and at the house, searching his soul. His eyes eventually land on the banker leaning against a fence post. Almost imperceptibly, the banker shakes his head and shrugs.

Tears mist Abigail's eyes. A single droplet spills over and trickles down her cheek.

"Going once ... going twice," the auctioneer threatens.

The distorted grin on Cromwell's face suddenly crumbles.

"Ten thousand." The cultured baritone carries easily across the yard. An impeccably dressed gentleman politely shoulders his way through the crowd, opening his arms to Abigail. "Hello Mother, you didn't think I'd let anyone steal away your dream, did you?"

More tears dribble down her cheeks as the joy of recognition blossoms in the warm sunshine. Abigail widens her smile and greets her son. A mouthful of bright, white teeth split his properly manicured beard and Justin sweeps Abigail into his arms.

"And you will dedicate a tiny corner in honor of investment gambling, won't you Mother?"

*** CONTRADICTION ***

When you know everything about a town, it's hard to keep its secrets. It's even harder to tell them and get it right ... so even those folks just passing through understand exactly how it is.   Each of us had at least a piece of the history but no one person knew it all, and it took years before the truth of it finally came out. The funeral helped, and all of us that went got a big part of the story that morning. Anyone that missed it then got told later by somebody else. As usual, embellishment stirred in a drop of its magic, if you want to call it that, then speculation simply filled in the holes. Always happens like that in a small town, you eventually get answers even if you don't ask.

Morgan James thought if he said nothing about it, nobody would figure he was the one that knocked Terry Madison's new Ford pick-up into the river one night when Morgan was driving home drunk from the Oak Creek Tavern.

Lucky for Terry he wasn't in it. Trouble was, everyone in town knew who did it, except Terry Madison, and nobody liked Terry so nobody told him. Nobody told him the next three times it happened either. Was getting to be the town joke, a continuous prank, knocking Terry's new pick-up truck into the creek.

Terry was a real obnoxious character, curling his lips and showing his teeth in a car salesman's grin every time he met anyone around town, always figuring an easy way to separate a stack of greenbacks from each person he met, even the few he mistakenly counted as friends.   Terry thought any dollar that ever touched his pocket remained his, even after he spent it. Always wanted it returned in the form of a new car purchase or periodic mechanical services for every vehicle the townsfolk owned, even if it had been originally bought elsewhere before Terry took over the auto business. Terry owned a lot of other stuff too, real estate and a factory, besides the Ford dealership that also sells tractors, seed, and farm equipment. His two older brothers still run the ranch, but Terry wanted nothing to do with cattle, never did like getting mud on his boots, even as a child.

The Madison Chip Factory employs over a hundred local folks. Terry had it built years ago on his portion of the family ranch beyond the north edge of Oak Creek after his old man died. The factory builds a special computer chip a national tool manufacturing company uses in its machines. Terry owned it and ran it, so nobody wanted to piss him off. Folks just never liked him much because he was obnoxious.

Terry couldn't help it, he simply didn't know any better. He mistakenly thought everyone wanted to hear about his successes, the people he'd gotten over on and put out of business so he could make more money with his endeavors. He thought they'd think just like he thought, and that he was very bright and business-wise. But actually Terry wasn't bright and business-wise, he just got lucky once in a while and was real good with numbers. It's a lot easier with a good inheritance too. Helps to begin already well on the way to rich.

And Terry was dead wrong about his personal image. Clever and astute were not terms the townsfolk used when talking about Terry, particularly after he'd given Hank Jacobson a personal loan to help him out with medical bills three years ago.

Hank and his wife Martie offered the Dodge dealership

as collateral, the only competition in town for Terry and his Fords. Terry really puffed his chest out about that gift for sixteen long months until Martie finally lost the battle.

Martie Jacobson drained all the money out of the company and spent the loan paying the hospital, the doctors, and the pharmacy while she fought cancer. Jacobson's dealership always made just enough money the last couple of years to carry the couple above the threshold for state and federal help.

Martie was a very feisty young woman, and tough. Been different if she'd been soft and had no heart, then she could've just given it up and the bills would've been less. Not Martie though, she'd fought for her life right up until the end and killed the family bank account doing it. Been different too if she'd just had a couple kids, a lot different though no one knew it at the time. Can't change that now.

Terry acted like he was such a great benefactor for waiting until she died to call the note. Actually waited until after the funeral, three days after it. Waited until Hank spent every dime he owned and then some, and wore out his tears too. Terry closed the Dodge lot the same weekend and then auctioned the inventory out-of-state. Moved both mechanics over to his Ford garage, then a month or so later he bulldozed the buildings. Hank went to live with his sister in Kansas. Took his wife with him in an urn.

After the Dodge lot closed, everyone local bought Fords or drove seventy-eight miles for a new Chevrolet, then seventy-eight miles for service, each way. Some did it just to spite Terry, but not many had that kind of time, especially if it meant taking a day off work and waiting in the service room to keep from having a friend make the same drive twice. And Terry, asshole that he was, wouldn't even service a new car if folks bought it in Dover Springs. Wanted all those dollars right back in his own pockets of course, but took an issue with neighbors that bought anything new or used but one of his Fords.

*

"Got to buy local," Terry always spouted after tipping a couple gins at the Tavern. Said it often enough too, every Friday evening in fact, including the last one, two days after he'd paid Shifty Ferguson to haul his Ford outta the river again. Shifty dripped into the tavern that Friday a little bit after Terry, wanting to spend some of the booty.

"Snake's coming up pretty good with all that water coming down off the hills. Probably crest in three or four days." Shifty announced it, as if nobody else had that information yet. But everyone knew it. Just common knowledge to all these farmers and ranchers – rains hard in the hills, river rises and floods its banks. Always happens.

Morgan James pushed into the bar right behind Shifty and shook the storm off his hat. "Evening folks, and you too Terry. Give yourself another new truck? Ought to git something besides a Ford, might last a while longer."

The words knocked the false grin off his face and Terry said, "Ef you, Morgan. Some low-life son-of-a-bee dumped my truck into the river again, didn't even stick around to tell me." Terry never used a real cuss word, just implied it with the first letter. Believed it made him classy. No one else thought so.

He slid a real grin back on his face that time though. "Sides, I ain't driving no seventy-eight miles each way to buy General Motors when I can git a free loaner all gassed up and washed every morning right over at Madison Ford, least 'til day after tomorrow when my new truck gits back on the road."

The grin slipped a bit when he thought about the truck, and the fact that he should have bought a tow truck last year so he wouldn't have had to pay Shifty Ferguson and his Texaco wrecker to haul him out. Four times this year, and he was getting tired of that bill. Maybe he should spring for AAA membership.

As if reading his mind, Morgan spoke again. "Maybe you ought to get yourself a AAA card, then they'd pay Shifty ... better yet, buy a tow truck and become a service rep for 'em. Then you could pay yourself to tow yourself." Everyone laughed at that one, including Terry.

"Good idea. Then I could get rich hiring stooges like you to knock me in the river so I could haul myself out and earn a fee. Never thought of that."

Everyone laughed again and Terry bought a round. Terry always bought a round when he told a joke, at least if the folks that heard it laughed. So everyone laughed when Terry joked, even if what he said wasn't funny. Everyone wanted his drink, and if you didn't laugh, he skipped over you.

Terry jotted a note on a small pad he kept in his shirt pocket, reminding himself about the AAA comment Morgan made. Terry always kept notes of the brilliant schemes he thought of – or ones others thought of – when he was drinking. Then he read them later to see if they had any merit. Most of them didn't, but Terry always took credit if it made sense, even if he never actually thought the idea up. He figured he contributed enough to claim it just by listening.

Most folks tolerated Terry and kept him company because he'd bought drinks and paid for lots of things around town. Two playgrounds and a town park have his name on a plaque at each entrance, a requirement to get his funds, among other things. He coached the town Little League team every year too, with few winners, but he'd also paid to have the baseball park built and kept it maintained.

Chatted the kids up all the time too while coaching, but nothing weird. He just loved kids, though had none of his own. No local woman could stand Terry enough days in a row to climb up on a mattress with him, let alone get serious.

About once a month or so he'd run over two counties and visit the Tart Room, a ninety -minute ride each way just to keep himself sane. Gals over there always drew straws to see who got rich old Terry whenever they heard he was coming. Short one lost and had to entertain him.

Terry even hit on Ginny Mae Crawford once. Sweet young gal only seventeen to his thirty-one, but naïve was not a term anyone except Terry used to describe Ginny Mae.

Word was Terry wanted to hook up and marry her before she knew better. Course, that's just Terry thinking his dumb social mistakes again.

Ginny Mae knew better long before Terry came chasing around, had already known better since she was about fourteen or so, no thanks to her cousins, and a little time spent hanging on a fence watching the stock bulls. Knew more'n Terry did probably, so he'd got shot down there too.

And lucky for Terry his three-day courtship began and ended in the middle of a hundred and eighty day package old Karl Crawford was spending with Sheriff Porky Barker for growing pot between the corn rows on his dairy farm. Otherwise Karl would have probably shot-gunned Terry for sniffing around his grand-daughter. Been the end of it right then, at least for Terry.

Had become an old wives-tale though by the time Karl got back home and started digging and planting again. So Terry was saved from that tragedy.

That's the Terry Madison everyone knew, or thought they knew. He had another side he shared with no one, at least no one in town, a very special side that even surprised

Terry when he thought enough about it. Seemed natural to him most of the time though, as natural as it had to his father. Each time Terry recalled it, the vision appeared in his mind unchanged, even after nineteen long years.

Framed by an antique gun collection hanging on the wall behind him, Morton Madison sat at his desk, a mahogany behemoth he'd hustled out of the principal's office years ago when Jefferson Tri-County built the new high school and demolished the old.

"Something you got to see son. Come along." Morton rose, tapped a Stetson down onto his ears, then walked outside and climbed into his new Ford Ranger.

Nearly two hours later, Morton and Terry accompanied headmistress Janice Springer along a hallway that fronted a line of open doors on ten separate rooms, each of which was home to a child. Some looked normal and some looked sick. But even the ones that looked normal were sick despite their appearance. But, they all stayed comfortable under the circumstances.

"They're all either terminal, or sick and homeless," Janice explained. "Your father maintains this clinic, and no one else knows where the money comes from."

The vision blurred and quickly shifted to a short bluff overlooking the Snake River outside Oak Creek, same bluff someone pushed Terry's truck over four times this past year or so. Father and son sat side-by-side in tan leather buckets, each sipping a beer.

"Why me, Morton?" Terry asked. Morton Madison insisted his boys call him by his given name. Made them feel his equal Morton always believed, and helped push his sons toward confidence and self-reliance.

"Made a mistake once, just once. Been paying for it ever since. Actually enjoy this place now. Found a passion here after all these years. You had a half-sister, came between you and your brothers. Weekend fling with a young gal used to work at Maggie's Cafe in town. Loved your mother then, always did, still do. Didn't know then what got into me, still don't. Youth and ignorance, couple whiskeys at the tavern, I'd guess. But I loved Ellie with all my heart, just couldn't break your mother's." A tear lit the corner of his eye.

"Ellie was born with some new kid's disease doctors had no cure for, still don't. Her mother give birth and run off, left her in the hospital. Told her I'd take care of her."

"Didn't believe me, I suppose. Scared and alone, with a sick child, no money. I bought this place and put Ellie in here with a full-time nurse. After awhile, a few other kids needed same kind of help. No place to go, nobody to keep 'em. Ellie struggled six years, happy as she could be given the situation. Never got old enough to know the difference. Added the north wing and just kept it going after that, helping kids that need it and have nothing."

Morton looked over at Terry. "You're my youngest. You got the job now. Kenny and Kurt run the ranch. Got no notion of this, maybe wouldn't even understand it. They both grew up to be cowboys. This always been a piece of the Ford business, nothing to do with the ranch. And, I'll be gone sooner than you think."

"Got to always remain ruthless in business Terry, every man for himself, take no prisoners. Adult against adult, man and his business got no rules, just make money. More money than anyone else, so you can carry this on. But never ever do nothing – even marginally – that will harm a child. That's my legacy to you. Continue my work at the shelter, but claim no credit for yourself."

Terry sat in the pick-up Shifty pulled out a couple weeks ago, right above the spot where it dropped in four times in a year. He thought about the other side of himself, the side no one knew about because he hid it, thought it might make him appear weak in front of the townsfolk. Besides, his father had sworn him to secrecy – protect the family name even after he's gone, protect his mother from the truth – so he couldn't tell even if he'd wanted.

Terry thrived upon the image he projected of a great, rich businessman, the cut-throat entrepreneur. But he spent a large portion of his profit on the kids health home his father founded and funded for children that had no way to survive without his help. He'd done it for eighteen years now, but thought it would make him look soft and easy, harm his business if he told. Another mistake. Plus, he'd promised his father. Can't hurt his mother, can't break a promise, especially a family promise. *"No fuckin' way!"* The actual swear word itself popped out into his mind for the first time ever, not just the first letter.

Terry always parked there once or twice a month, the nights he visited the shelter, the same bluff overlooking the Snake, same bluff where his father explained his life.

Janice always picked him up in a Buick he bought new for her every couple years in Dover Springs, and sent back there three times a year for maintenance. Never wanted anyone to see his truck at the clinic, and never wanted a free Ford to tie Janice back to Terry and the dealership.

He'd taken a rest after a particularly brutal night at the shelter. One of the sickest kids had an extremely difficult time and finally given up her soul. He'd nodded his head on the wheel for a moment after Janice dropped him off and fell asleep in his truck before he got started home.

An hour or so later, Shifty Ferguson passed behind the new Ford with a half-empty pint stuck between his knees. Decided it was his turn once again to continue the game. He'd backed up then pushed Terry's pick-up over the edge with the very same tow truck he'd used to drag it out the last time, and fully expected to drag it out with again this time.

Shifty chuckled quietly and raced off to tell the townsfolk he'd pushed Terry's truck into the water again, let 'em laugh about it behind Terry's back one more time. Besides, Shifty figured it got him a little bit even for what Terry done to his sister and Hank.

Many speculate but no one knows for sure what his last thoughts might have been when Terry and his Ford slid into the river. Most of us that knew him want to believe the final image that crossed his mind as Terry breathed in water while struggling to open the truck door against the pressure of the flow was one of Martie Jacobson and how he could have helped her if only she'd just borne a child or two.

The townsfolk never would have known about that secret side of Terry Madison either, except he'd been unlucky and sitting inside his pick-up the last time it fell into the Snake. Unlucky too that it happened after a heavy rain breached its banks. Otherwise, he'd have got into water up just above the wheel wells like the other four times.

Truth came out though. Janice Springer showed up at his funeral and told the family and a few guests what Terry Madison had been doing all those years. After awhile, everyone in town knew it.

Visitors that stop to eat or sight-see while passing through Oak Creek often ask about the bronze statue surrounded by flowers that sits in the town square but has no name, just the way Terry Madison would have wanted. Sometimes we tell the story, sometimes not, depends on the day, and who's asking. But no one ever rats on Shifty, everyone says the brakes just let go, and Terry's truck simply rolled off the bluff and he drowned.